ELF
ELEMENTARY

ELF ELEMENTARY

ELF ELEMENTARY

By Edward Miller

Harry N. Abrams, Inc., Publishers

Today is my first day at elf school. Our teacher Ms. Tinsel calls attendance.

"Is Franklin present?" she asks.

"Here I am!" I say.

"Let's begin," says Ms. Tinsel. "Welcome to your first day at Elf Elementary. If you pass all your classes you will meet Santa Claus and ride in his sleigh."

Oh, I want to ride in Santa's sleigh so bad. I better study real hard.

We all get a uniform to wear. Mine is a little small but I don't mind—I'm excited to have my first red elf suit!

LOCKER
ROOMS
▶

GIRLS

The first recorded celebration of Christmas was in Rome in 336. That's over 1600 years ago.

The word **CHRISTMAS** comes from an 11th-century term meaning **CHRIST'S MASS.**

BOYS

Christmas is the celebration of the birth of Jesus Christ. Christians believe that the birth occurred in a manger in Bethlehem. Shepherds and three kings came to witness the event. Many Christians have in their homes a replica of the manger called a crèche, complete with sheep.

Stars are a popular Christmas symbol representing the Star of Bethlehem which led the three kings to where Jesus was born. A star is often placed on top of Christmas trees for decoration.

Season's Greetings

NOEL!

Noel is the French word for Christmas. It comes from the Latin word meaning birthday.

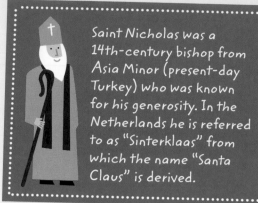

Saint Nicholas was a 14th-century bishop from Asia Minor (present-day Turkey) who was known for his generosity. In the Netherlands he is referred to as "Sinterklaas" from which the name "Santa Claus" is derived.

JOY!

● Room 101

Xmas Ca...
Christmas Lights
Ornaments

Candles represent Jesus, who is referred to as the light of the world. They also symbolize longing for the sun in the dark of winter.

Angels play a big part in the Christmas story. Christians believe that the angel Gabriel told Mary that she would give birth to Jesus. Angels also announced the birth to shepherds in nearby fields who went to worship the newborn baby.

Happy Holidays

HAPPY HOLIDAYS!

Room 102

I pick up my books and supplies and hurry to class. It will be a busy day—I have a lot to learn and a lot to carry.

Tree Trimming is the first class.

"The custom of decorating trees began in Germany 400 years ago," notes Ms. Tinsel. "Some trees were decorated with apples, paper roses, and candies. Franklin, remember you're decorating the tree, not yourself!"

Nabisco started making Barnum's Animal Crackers in 1902. The box's carrying string was designed for hanging on the tree.

In New York City, Rockefeller Center's Christmas tree has about five miles of lights on it. The first tree was put up by construction workers in 1931 when the Center was being built. It remains a tradition to this day.

Queen Victoria and Prince Albert made decorating Christmas trees a popular custom in England in the 1840s.

In the 1930s the Addis Brush Company made artificial trees based on a toilet brush they made.

When Theodore Roosevelt was president, he barred Christmas trees from the White House to help preserve the forests, encouraging Americans to do the same.

Candles were used on trees until the electric light bulb was invented in 1879 by Thomas Edison.

The first American president to have a tree in the White House was Franklin Pierce in 1856.

In the library we discover many fascinating books about Christmas.

"May I read *A Christmas Carol?*" says Peppermint.

"No, I'm keeping that book—it's my favorite," I answer.

"A scrooge is someone who doesn't share," says Ms. Tinsel. "Do you want to be the class scrooge?"

"On second thought, you can borrow it, Peppermint."

Clement Clarke Moore, a scholar and poet from New York City, wrote "The Night Before Christmas" in 1821, for his children. It became a popular tale in America and describes what most Americans have come to believe about Santa Claus.

Hans Christian Andersen, a Dutch author, wrote many fairy tales with Christmas themes, such as "The Steadfast Tin Soldier" in 1838, about a one-legged tin soldier and a paper ballerina who find true love.

The Steadfast Tin Soldier

English novelist Charles Dickens wrote *A Christmas Carol* in 1843. It's a story about a stingy man named Ebenezer Scrooge. He is visited by three spirits on Christmas Eve who teach him charity and kindness. From this book came the term "scrooge" to mean a person who is selfish.

Quiet Please!

American writer Washington Irving wrote *Diedrich Knickerbocker's History of New York from the Beginning of the World to the End of the Dutch Dynasty* in 1809. In this book Americans were introduced to Saint Nicholas as a bearer of gifts at Christmastime.

The Night Before Christmas

The Little Match Girl

The Fir Tree

W. IRVING

Cookie Class makes me hungry. We learn to decorate all kinds of cookies.

"Hey, you're doing it all wrong!" exclaims Twinkle. "Witches, pumpkins, and ghosts are for Halloween—not Christmas."

Oh drats!

I try to cover them up with plenty of sprinkles before Ms. Tinsel can see.

If I don't pass this class I won't meet Santa.

Geography Class is the hardest one—so many places to remember! "You'll need to know your way around the world if you want to travel with Santa Claus on Christmas Eve," says Ms. Tinsel. "Franklin, perhaps you would like to travel back to your seat and follow along."

Dasher

Dancer

French-Canadian folklore is rich with stories of the supernatural, with tales about werewolves, ghost canoes, and phantoms. One popular legend tells how the dead return to hear Mass at midnight on Christmas Eve and to look again on their homes.

In New York City Santa rides his sled down Broadway in the Macy's Thanksgiving Day Parade.

In Idaho ancestors of the Basque shepherds attend the Sheepherders Ball.

In Washington, D.C., the president lights the nation's Christmas tree across from the White House.

NORTH AMERICA

In Hawaii Santa arrives in a canoe.

In Texas cowboys attend a dance called the Cowboys' Christmas Ball, first held in 1885.

In New Orleans people ignite bonfires along the Mississippi River to light the way for Santa.

In Brazil Santa visits with thousands of children in Maracaña Stadium to sing carols. He arrives by helicopter.

In Mexico blindfolded children smash open piñatas filled with small toys and candy.

SOUTH AMERICA

In Argentina many families spend Christmas Day at the beach because it's warm in December.

N
W ◄ ► E
S

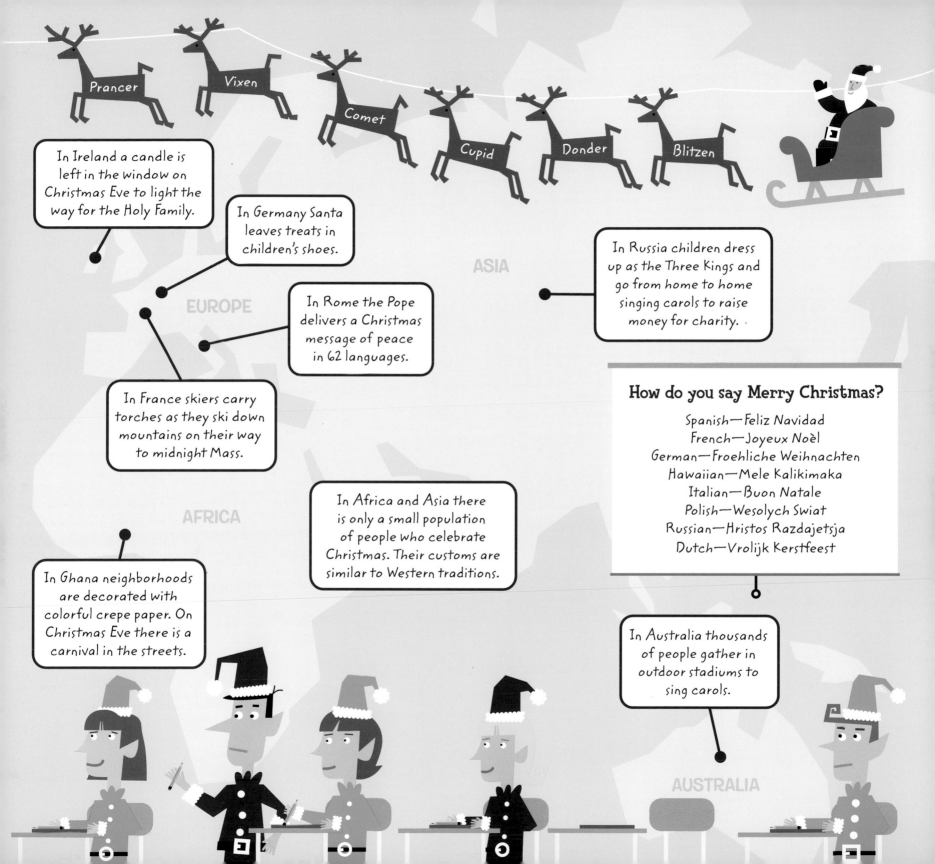

Prancer

Vixen

Comet

Cupid

Donder

Blitzen

In Ireland a candle is left in the window on Christmas Eve to light the way for the Holy Family.

In Germany Santa leaves treats in children's shoes.

ASIA

In Russia children dress up as the Three Kings and go from home to home singing carols to raise money for charity.

EUROPE

In Rome the Pope delivers a Christmas message of peace in 62 languages.

In France skiers carry torches as they ski down mountains on their way to midnight Mass.

AFRICA

In Africa and Asia there is only a small population of people who celebrate Christmas. Their customs are similar to Western traditions.

In Ghana neighborhoods are decorated with colorful crepe paper. On Christmas Eve there is a carnival in the streets.

How do you say Merry Christmas?

Spanish—Feliz Navidad
French—Joyeux Noèl
German—Froehliche Weihnachten
Hawaiian—Mele Kalikimaka
Italian—Buon Natale
Polish—Wesolych Swiat
Russian—Hristos Razdajetsja
Dutch—Vrolijk Kerstfeest

In Australia thousands of people gather in outdoor stadiums to sing carols.

AUSTRALIA

There is a legend that says that Saint Nicholas gave gold pieces to three daughters of a poor man to use as a dowry so they could marry and live respectable lives. The gold was secretly placed in their stockings—starting the tradition of leaving gifts in stockings.

In England children send their wish lists to Father Christmas by burning them in the fireplace. The smoke carries their wishes to him.

In Holland, Black Pete (Saint Nicholas's helper), goes down the chimney first to keep St. Nicholas from getting his clothes dirty.

In Scotland, on Christmas Eve, children shout their wishes up the chimney for Father Christmas to hear.

After lunch is Gym. We race through an obstacle course. Our team comes in last because I get stuck in the chimney chute.

"Franklin, you'll have to practice until you get it right," says Ms. Tinsel. "You don't want to get stuck on Christmas Eve."

"Can't I use the front door?" I ask.

"Oh, Franklin, you know that's the easy way out, or, in this case, the easy way in!" chuckles Ms. Tinsel.

Next is Music Class. "The word 'carol' comes from an ancient Greek word meaning to circle-dance with singing," says Ms. Tinsel.

I bet Ms. Tinsel is glad she chose me to sing a solo because I can sing real loud.

The song "White Christmas" was written and composed by Irving Berlin in 1940 and sung by Bing Crosby in the movie *Holiday Inn* in 1942. It won the Oscar for best song that year.

OSCAR

Production Manager: Jonathan Lopes

Library of Congress Cataloging-in-Publication Data

Miller, Edward, 1964–
Elf Elementary / by Edward Miller.
p. cm.
Summary: Franklin is excited to be a student at an elementary school for elves, where he studies Christmas traditions, geography, how to get through soot, and other lessons as he prepares to be a Christmas elf.
ISBN 0-8109-8721-X (alk. paper)
[1. Elves—Fiction. 2. Schools—Fiction. 3. Christmas—Fiction. 4. Santa Claus—Fiction.] I. Title.

PZ7.M61287El 2004
[Fic]—dc22
2004001462

Printed and bound in China
10 9 8 7 6 5 4 3 2 1

Harry N. Abrams, Inc.
100 Fifth Avenue
New York, NY 10011
www.abramsbooks.com

Abrams is a subsidiary of

LA MARTINIÈRE
GROUPE

MERRY CHRISTMAS!

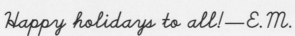

Happy holidays to all!—E.M.

I jump on just as the sleigh is taking off.

"Dash away, dash away, dash away *now!*" I shout.

"Ho! Ho! Ho! That's dash away, dash away, dash away *all!*" says Santa in a deep voice.

I guess I still have a lot to learn.

I can hardly believe my pointy ears: I *passed!*

I quickly run for Santa's sleigh.

"No running in the halls!" Ms. Tinsel calls out after me.

Then Ms. Tinsel adds, "But you certainly showed the most improvement. I'm happy to say you passed! You tried your best and may ride with Santa."

One by one Ms. Tinsel hands out the report cards. She's getting closer and closer to me. So far everyone has passed.

"Franklin had trouble with most of his studies," says Ms. Tinsel in front of everyone.

My heart sinks.

And then the party ends. "Okay, class, please line up. I'm handing out the report cards now," says Ms. Tinsel.

I'm the last one in line.

I'm *so* nervous!

Legend says the candy cane was invented by the choirmaster of Cologne Cathedral in France in the 1670s. He had peppermint candies made in the shape of a shepherd's staff to keep the children quiet during church services.

Mistletoe has a long history and association with Christmas. Celtic priests believed the plant was sacred and that it could cure illnesses and protect against evil spirits. If enemies met under mistletoe in a forest they would call a truce until the next day, thus making the plant a symbol of peace. From this came the custom of hanging mistletoe and kissing under it as a sign of friendship and goodwill.

Gingerbread houses are a common decoration at Christmas and a tasty treat. Gingerbread has been baked in Europe for centuries. The idea of molding gingerbread into houses comes from the German fairy tale "Hansel and Gretel," where the children discover a house made of bread and candies.

There are lots of gifts and goodies at the party. I almost forget how nervous I am about my report card when I find a cool red fire truck with a siren under the tree for me.

An evergreen wreath symbolizes life in winter when the earth is cold and barren.

Ms. Tinsel   Joy   Ginger   Jingle   Holly   Twinkle   Franklin   Peppermint   Frost

The poinsettia plant was named after Joel R. Poinsett (1779—1851), an American congressman and ambassador to Mexico. He brought back the popular Christmas plant from Mexico on his return to the United States.

F.D.

7 Swans a-swimming

8 Maids a-milking

9 Ladies dancing

10 Lords a-leaping

11 Pipers piping

12 Drummers drumming

This counting song dates back to the 1500s when it was customary to exchange a gift on each of the twelve days.

Oo Pp Qq Rr Ss Tt Uu Vv Ww Xx Yy Zz

Reindeer on the rooftop was first introduced by Clement Clarke Moore in "The Night Before Christmas," a poem which likely inspired this song written in 1860.

"Up on the Housetop" by Benjamin R. Handy

Up on the housetop reindeer pause,
Out jumps good old Santa Claus;
Down thro' the chimney with lots of toys,
All for the little ones'
Christmas joys

Ho, ho, ho!
Who wouldn't go!
Ho, ho, ho!
Who wouldn't go!
Up on the housetop
Click, click, click
Down thro' the chimney with
Good Saint Nick.

Supplies:
hat
scarf
carrot
coal
twigs
snow

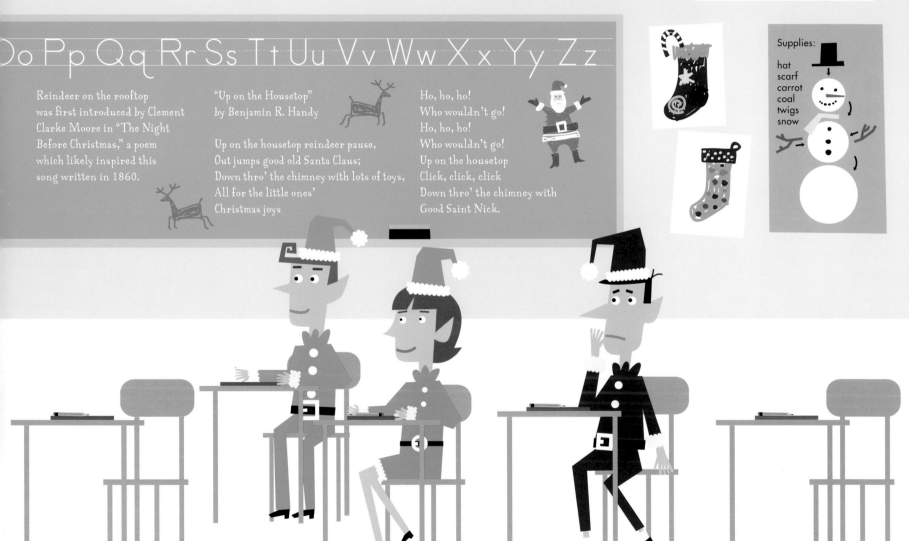

having a Christmas Eve Party, and then I'll hand out your report cards. Those of you who pass will go for a ride in Santa's sleigh before he leaves on his big trip."
Oh, I sure hope I pass.

The Twelve Days of Christmas are from Christmas Day to the Epiphany, the day the three kings arrived in Bethlehem.

 1 | Partridge in a pear tree
 2 Turtledoves
 3 French hens
 4 Calling birds
 5 Golden rings
 6 Geese-a-laying

No Homework Today!

CHRISTMAS PARTY! TOMORROW

Aa Bb Cc Dd Ee Ff Gg Hh Ii Jj Kk Ll Mm N

The weeks pass. There are sure a lot of things to learn before you can become a Christmas elf.

Then one day Ms. Tinsel makes an announcement. "Tomorrow we're

The first United States Christmas stamp was issued in 1962. It was a four-cent stamp with a picture of a wreath.

About two and a half billion Christmas cards are mailed each Christmas in the United States alone. That's a whole lot!

The last class of the day is Art. We make greeting cards and decorate gift boxes.

"Did you know that in 1236 King Louis IX of France gave King Henry III of England a live elephant as a Christmas present?" says Holly.

"Really? How did he wrap it?" I joke.

From,
Ike & Mamie

Dwight D. Eisenhower was the first American president to send out official presidential Christmas cards, in 1953.

Ms. Andrea
25 Merry Lane
UT 94849

Cousin Linas
50 Chestnut Ave.
KA 80541

Susan
est 18 St.
0010

During the Middle Ages carols were sung between scenes at Christmas plays for entertainment. When the play was over the singing continued in the streets, starting the practice of street caroling.

In 1850, "Jingle Bells" was written by composer James S. Pierpont. During the Civil War he was a Confederate soldier who wrote rallying songs.

In 1816, Father Joseph Mohr, an Austrian priest, wrote "Silent Night." He was inspired to write the poem after traveling in the snow at night to bless a mother and her newborn baby. The poem was later set to music.

Gene Autry, also known as the "singing cowboy," wrote "Here Comes Santa Claus" in 1946. He also sang "Rudolph the Red-Nosed Reindeer" in 1949, and "Frosty the Snowman" in 1950. Autry was a popular movie and TV performer.